This Boxer Book paperback belongs to

. . . .

www.boxerbooks.com

Clip-Clop

Nicola Smee

Boxer Books

"Who wants a ride?"
asks Mr Horse.

"Me, please," says Cat.

Clip-clop, clippity-clop...

"I want a ride too,
please Mr Horse," says Dog.

"Up you get,"
says Mr Horse.

"Whoa! Stop!
We're falling off!"

squeal Cat and Dog
and Pig and Duck.

Mr Horse skids to a
HALT!

And Cat
and Dog
and Pig
and Duck

f l y through the air...

... and land in a haystack.

Plop!
Plop!
Ploppity-

"Oh dear!
Oh dear!
Oh dearie me!"
says worried Mr Horse.

"Ag

ain!"

cry Cat
and Dog
and Pig
and Duck.

"Up you get!" laughs Mr Horse.

And Cat and Dog and Pig
and Duck go riding off again.

Clip-clop,

clippity-clop!

For CHROME HOOF
Nicola Smee

First published in Great Britain in 2006
by Boxer Books Limited.
www.boxerbooks.com

Hardback ISBN 1-905417-03-9
Paperback ISBN 1-905417-04-7

3 5 7 9 10 8 6 4 2

Printed in Slovenia

Other Boxer Books paperbacks

Chicky Chicky Chook Chook: Cathy MacLennan

Chicky chicks, buzzy bees and kitty cats romp in sun and snuggle in the warmth, until pitter-patter, down comes the rain. A great read-aloud, sing-along book, full of fun-to-imitate animal sounds, rhythm and movement.

ISBN 13: 978-1-905417-32-2

Ha Ba, Baby!: Kate Petty & Georgie Birkett

Ha Ha, Baby! is the story of one very grumpy baby. Just how far will this family go to make their little one laugh? A fun family tale of clowning around.

ISBN 13: 978-1-905417-16-2

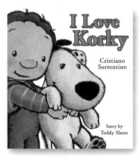

I Love Korky: Cristiano Sorrentino

Korky is the loveable, huggable and ever so snuggle-able puppy that all young children will adore. With appealing art and fun, read-aloud text, this book is perfect for sharing with little ones.

ISBN 13: 978-1-905417-83-4

Tip Tip Dig Dig: Emma Garcia

Tip Tip Dig Dig is a bright and inventive story for children. Each construction vehicle makes its own noise as they all work together towards a surprise ending. Perfect for reading aloud.

ISBN 13: 978-1-905417-84-1